Fatso in the Red Suit

Matthew Sweeney was born in Donegal in 1952 and has lived in London since 1973. He works increasingly in schools, both primary and secondary, encouraging children to write, and has two children of his own. In 1994/5 he was Poet in Residence at London's South Bank Centre. He also writes for adults.

MATTHEW SWEENEY

Fatso in the Red Suit

illustrated by David Austen

faber and faber
LONDON · BOSTON

First published in 1995
by Faber and Faber Limited
3 Queen Square London WC1N 3AU

This paperback edition first published in 1996

Photoset by Wilmaset, Birkenhead, Wirral
Printed and bound in Great Britain by
Mackays of Chatham PLC, Chatham, Kent

A CIP record for this book is
available from the British Library

ISBN 0-571-17903-7

2 4 6 8 10 9 7 5 3 1

for Nico and Malvin

Contents

Fatso in the Red Suit

It was October
and already the fake Santas
were filling the grottos
in the big stores,
and here was one on the telly
in a false white beard,
fat, like they always were,
his red-covered belly
bursting like he'd eaten a turkey
by himself, his voice
yo-ho-ho gruff,
his grin showing in each eye.
And Dave was on the sofa,
watching, with Dad beside him
sipping a glass of red wine
then choking on a guffaw
as he pointed at the screen,
'Would you look at him,
that Fatso in the Red Suit,'
and Dave turned green.

'Fatso in the Red Suit'
his Dad continued, singing it
to the beat of his foot,

'Fatso, Fatso in the Red Suit',
till Dave jumped up
and switched the telly off,
then turned to his Dad
and begged him to stop.
'He's not Fatso,' he shouted.
'He's Santa Claus.
You're almost as fat as he is.'
And Dave almost got clouted
but he carried on,
'He's not the real Santa
but he's still a bit of a Santa.
He's good, and you're mean,
and if you keep calling him
Fatso in the Red Suit,
he won't come here this year
and he'll do you harm.'

*

Over the next few weeks
Dave's Dad continued to sneer
at anything he'd see or hear
about Santa. And there were lots
of Fatsos in Red Suits about,
though Dave never called them that.
And each time his Dad did
Dave left the room. It happened

that Dad and Mum were fighting,
not about Fatsos in Red Suits,
about their own business. Every night
as Dave sat in bed reading
he'd hear them upstairs, shouting
at each other. Then one morning
Dad packed his bag and left
and Dave immediately blamed himself.

*

No word from Dad for days,
no luck ringing friends of his.

Mum moping in her room,
or saying he'd be back soon.

Dave watching things on telly
even he knew were silly.

Dave sad with no Dad,
thinking of the laughs they had,

wishing he knew where Dad was,
thinking: 'Dad, come home to us.'

Then, a message on the ansaphone –
Dad, for Dave, not Mum,

saying, 'Miss you more each day.'
To Dave he sounded far away.

*

Dave started to dream,
he dreamed five nights in a row,
then he stopped for two,
and dreamed five nights more.

He dreamed his Dad
was up in northern Iceland
working for a skinny man
who owned a toy factory.

Each of Dave's dreams
led into the next, like chapters
in a book, and in each
was Dave's Dad and the skinny man

who was also a stubbled man
and a grumpy man, and called
Dave's Dad Peter,
and didn't seem to like children.

Or that's how the first dream
showed it. And Dave's Dad
didn't like children either,
though Dave knew this was a lie.

In Dave's second dream
he heard the man being called
Mr Christmas, and saw
it wasn't children he disliked,

only naughty children,
of which there were plenty, he said,
and Dave's Dad had the job
of haunting the dreams of these.

Dave woke up at this,
but he didn't feel haunted.
His Dad wasn't in his dreams
nearly enough, but Mr Christmas was.

On the third night
Dave dreamed the painted sign
above the factory door –
it said *Sinte Klass*.

And he began to notice
the changing look of Mr Christmas,
his beard was thick now
though he was still skinny.

And each night his clothes
were different, from jeans
to a bishop's suit. And now
Dave's Dad called him Nick.

Dave's two dreamless nights
were needed for resting,
but he did a lot of thinking
and almost told his Mum.

The sixth dream was in colour
and Mr Christmas was in green,
while Dave's Dad was in black
as both peered into a book.

The dream went in close-up.
It was a notebook, with lists
of the naughty children
and Dave saw his name there.

Mr Christmas was drinking beer
in dream seven, and Dad
was handing him a cigar,
and they'd both put on weight.

And Mr Christmas would change clothes
in mid-dream, from blue
to brown, to any colour, as if
he was looking for the right colour.

And the toys kept mounting
at the back of the factory,
each with a tab that matched
a name in a second notebook.

Dave couldn't read these
and the last dreams didn't help —
they were jumbled, and strange
and all took place on Christmas Eve,

(still weeks away) when bees
hummed psalms at midnight,
and animals could talk
and angels sang in pine trees,

and Mr Christmas rode among them
on a white horse, pulling a cart
full of toys, his beard white now
and him fat and wearing red.

*

When the dreams stopped
Dave wrote a letter,
he addressed it 'Mr Christmas',
made a photocopy,
sent one to Greenland,
the other to Iceland.

He wrote 'Dear Mr Christmas,
I don't want any toys,
I want my Dad –
the man you call Peter
who dresses in black.
I want him back.'

*

It was mid-December
when Dave got a letter
from his Dad,
from the north of England,
enclosing a photo
of him in a grotto
in a red suit
and falsely fat.

He said to tell Mum
he'd be home
for Christmas,
and he'd bring lots –
a turkey
and brandy
and as many toys
as he'd fit on the bus.

And on Christmas Eve
as they made to leave
for church
he stood on the porch
in his red suit
looking *really* fat –
Dave's Dad was home
and Santa had still to come.

My Party

Come to my party on Christmas Eve
in my rented air balloon.
Well, it's really a Zeppelin,
and at midnight you've got to leave.

Why? Because it's Christmas.
How do you get up there?
Hitch a ride on a helicopter.
Do it, and don't make a fuss,

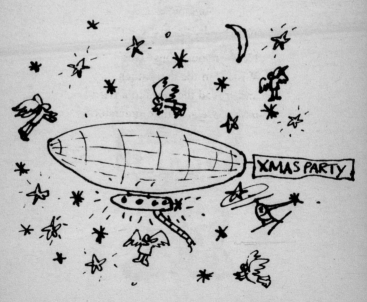

and don't be late, or the angels
won't appear in their feathers
or their spacesuit evening wear,
and the food will go to the gulls.

The food? There'll be larks' eggs
and flying fish, and roast crow.
(Horrible? How do you know?)
And specially imported moon figs.

Oh, and coke made with rain.
What about music? The stars
helped along by meteors
will cobble together a tune.

No more questions? Good.
Write it in the diary, then,
and spread the news to a friend
immediately. Is that understood?

The Silent Knight

He went into a huff at Christmas,
there in the crowded church
with the choir behind him, singing hymns
about kings, and mangers
and a holy, silent *night*!

So he became a silent *knight*,
and stormed from the church
to don his armour, mount his horse
and head for his castle home
where he brooded in the bedroom

then pinned up a notice
sacking all the servants,
advertising for dumb replacements,
and warning his wife
never to speak to him again.

And each month at the joust
he was invincible,
his lance became a tin-opener
leaving the meat of knights
for maggots to gobble,

while he never boasted
or cried out in triumph,
just galloped home to his silent castle
where harpists were barred
and monks went on the fire.

Grandpa's Monkeys

My maternal Grandpa was a sailor
    who, back in the 1920s,
    took an unnatural fancy
to that sheer rock called Gibraltar.

The women there were half-Spanish,
    had black eyes, wore little,
    but Grandpa couldn't settle
with any female, except the ape-ish

ones who hung from the rock's face
    with one hand, and squealed
    at any ship that wheeled
into the Straits at an iceberg's pace.

And he brought one home, did Gramps,
    to our gawping Cardiff street,
    with black shoes on its feet,
and they both died of the same mumps.

Vanya and the Kid

I am Vanya.
I sell hot dogs in Idaho Falls.
I serve my own mustard,
and it is *good* mustard,
good *Russian* mustard –
the kid eats it with bread.

The kid? Kurt
he calls himself in his funny accent
on the odd times he speaks.
He's gone now, South somewhere,
I don't know where. Took
off three weeks back.

You know him?
You say his name's Jurgen?
So, what's in a name?
He's a *good* kid, no trouble
to no one. Now he's gone.

Took with him
the monkey, rattlesnake and skunk
that shared his room
while he slept in the bath.
You looking for him?

If you find him bring him back.

Rio

The kid's in Rio
I know, I know,
and we can't climb lampposts together,
can't hang up there
and yodel, till the whole street's out
and we're running,
laughing, yelling
through the park, raising pigeon storms.

But now he's in Rio
I can't climb lampposts alone.

The kid's in Rio
I know, I know
from my South American dream,
of Copacabana
and maracas, and glimpses of the kid
in the harbour,
in the churned bay,
on a skateboard through the streets.

The packed streets of Rio
that I can't afford to reach.

Moon Golf

The boy on the side of the mountain
points a telescope at the moon.
He's heard there's a golfball up there
since 1969
and he hopes to glimpse it soon.

He moves his lens in a slow arc
and sees craters, pocky craters.
The ball must be up there somewhere.
That astronaut was some golfer.
Imagine hitting a ball that far.

The boy himself is a golfer.
He plays every day in summer –
he played once at dawn
and one of these days he'll paint
a golfball luminous green

and head off down at midnight,
with the telescope in his bag
(between the 9 iron and the putter),
ready to point at the moon
the first time he replaces the flag.

A Boy

Half a mile from the sea,
in a house with a dozen bedrooms
he grew up. Who was he?
Oh, nobody much. A boy
with the usual likes
and more than a few dislikes.
Did he swim much? Nah,
that sea was the Atlantic
and out there is *Ice*land.
He kept his play inland
on an L-shaped football pitch
between the garage and the gate.
What did he eat?
Stuff his grandfather made,
home-made sausages,
potted pig's head.
He got the library keys
and carried eight books at a time
home, and he read.
He read so much
he stayed in the book's world.
Wind rattled the window
of his third-storey room,
but his bed was warm.

And he stayed in his bed
half the day if he could,
reading by candlelight
when the storms struck
and the electricity died.
How do I know all this?
You'd guess how if you tried.

Cornered

Stand in the corner, John.
Put that dunce's hat on.
Don't even think of turning round –
you're there till home-time, my son,
and longer, if you make a single sound.

What did you do, John?
You know very well, my son.
And stop grinning, the rest of you.
You think this is a piece of fun?
You think I wouldn't swap John for you?

Stop smirking, John.
You're unlike anyone
I've ever met in a classroom.
You're subnormal, my son.
What do you ever do when you're at home?

Don't answer that, John.
And keep the dunce's hat on.
I just might stick it on with glue.
It looks cute on you, my son.
I've plenty stored away for the rest of you.

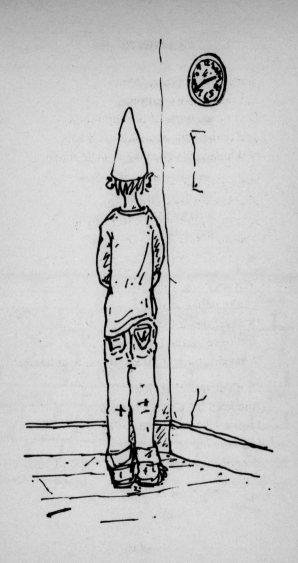

Only the Wall

That first day
only the wall saw
the bully
trip the new boy
behind the shed,
and only the wall heard
the name he called,
a name that would stick
like toffee.

The second day
the wall didn't see
the fight
because too many
boys stood around,
but the wall heard
their cheers,
and no one cheered for
the new boy.

The third day
the wall felt
three bullies
lean against it,
ready to ambush
the new boy,
then the wall heard
thumps and cries,
and saw blood.

The fourth day
only the wall missed
the new boy
though five bullies
looked for him,
then picked another boy
instead. Next day

they had him back,
his face hit the wall.

The sixth day
only the wall knew
the bullies
would need that other boy
to savage.
The wall remembered
the new boy's face
going home,
saw he'd stay away.

The New Boy

The new boy has many names,
or no name he likes enough to keep.
He comes from Romania, or Austria,
or Hungary, or Albania.
He's a cracker, he's funny, he's a creep.
He has pet bats in his roof garden,
and a pickled dead scorpion,
and he hangs up the skeletons of fish.
He's carving a sarcophagus
out of ebony, and he says
he'll sail in it down the canal.
He likes air balloons, too,
and he wears big-brimmed hats.
Sometimes we're not sure we hear
him right, as his accent's strong,
but seeing as his Dad's the undertaker
we can't be completely wrong.

Off School

As the doctor asked him to,
he rinsed his throat with vinegar
then ate a bag of kumquats.
And soon the bugs had decomposed,
so he banged his bedroom door,
then hurried down the stairs.
Where was he escaping to?
Not school! Great Crikes, the thought!
He was heading for the park, of course,
with his scarf around his neck,
and underneath his jacket
a football. Would he play alone?
You bet! Unless you count the ducks
he curved those corners to,
or the sheep whose heads he found
when he floated free-kicks in,
or the drunk he just persuaded
to sway around in goal.
And what more useful way to spend
a well-earned day off school?

Ned's Will

My Uncle Ned died last week.
He wasn't my favourite
but he is now, and my Mum
when she hears Ned's name
chokes back a gollop of spit.

My Dad finds this funny, and says
he must have been wrong about Ned.
Mum and he aren't speaking.
She's showing few signs of grieving
for her brother who's barely dead.

What has Ned done to upset her?
Nothing, as far as I can see.
He left her his palomino
and a stuffed head of a buffalo
but he left his farm to me.

My Mum asked if I'd like to swap.
I thought about it, but no –
I can't ride, and what would I do
with the stuffed head of a buffalo?
So I said to my Mum, 'No go.'

We all flew out for the funeral.
That was before the will.
As we stood while the lawyer spoke
I thought my Mum would choke.
I can see her face still.

My Dad took me out to the farm
while Mum sulked in a bar.
We drove through a canyon
and past a goldmine,
and I figured I'd need a car.

Dad could teach me to drive it.
I already knew how to steer.
I looked out at sheep and cattle
and at trees on the hills
and I knew I'd like it here.

I liked the farmhouse already.
I'd build a windmill beside it
and I'd ring it with cacti
and I'd open the roof to the sky,
but even as it was I liked it.

And all those steers were mine.
Good burgers. I'd grow corn, too,
and I'd try a few orange trees
and maybe I'd keep bees,
at least a hive or two.

Dad could come and live with me,
Mum as well. She'd forget the will.
We'll sell this flat in London
and move to Arizona, soon.
But first I'll finish school.

After Dinner

After the mad dinner party
when Mum ate nothing
and Dad ate everything,
saying it was his birthday,
and everyone drank a lot
(including my sister who's twelve —
she kept on helping herself),
so much that Mum and Dad fought,
till everyone went home,
leaving my sister to weep
while tired-out Mum fell asleep
and Dad sat there, glum —
after all this I invented
a language for bored boys,
something instead of toys,
to keep me and my kind contented
when people come to dine,
people who bypass us
unless we create a fuss
or they're too full with wine.
I call this language *Splat*
and only boys can learn it,
boys who've had to sit
through mad dinners like that.

I'll teach you a few words —
belush means bullshit,
stram means quit,
go home, wake the birds.
I'm not saying anymore
in case you're not boys.
I've had it with dinner noise.
Fhlorr means sore!

Honey

The bee buzzed over the honey pot
left open on the table.
'That's mine,' he thought, 'not theirs!
They're as bad as grizzly bears.
I'm going to steal it back if I'm able.'

He hovered and buzzed and dipped
below the rim of the pot
till he could sniff and smell his fill.
It was foreign honey, but still.
Home in the hive there wasn't a lot.

He buzzed in a figure-of-eight
and dodged the sticky spoon.
He flew up and landed on the rim.
How would he get the honey home?
He'd better hurry. They'd be back soon.

Should he go to the hive for help?
Bring a swarm back
to carry each sweet drop at once,
with a dozen bees hanging loose
to guard in case of attack?

He buzzed down to the honey again.
He'd better taste it first.
Who knew what had been done with it?
Boiled, or stuff mixed in with it?
They were known to do their worst.

He landed gently on the meniscus.
He dipped a claw inside
and brought a sticky drop to his mouth.
Six out of ten, he'd tasted worse.
It was time he headed for the hive.

But when he flapped his papery wings
he saw he was stuck there.
He flapped so hard he began to hum.
He telepathized the Queen to come
but he stayed stuck there

till a boy came in and found him,
and pulled his wings off
and squeezed him till he was dead
then spread him, with honey, on bread –
over half a French loaf

which the boy gave to his sister
as they sat down to tea,
and the boy crumbled a bee wing
while the girl swallowed a bee sting.
'Mmn,' she said. 'Wonderful honey!'

The Red House

sits in the elm tree
like a nest —
a square, red nest
made of wood.

It would float away if it could.

Its one window
faces north,
the dangerous north.
It has no door —

just a square hole in the floor.

Who lives there?
A monkey,
a red monkey
with no tail —

like a yacht without a sail.

And every evening
a boy,
a blond boy
stands below

to shout into the tree HELLO.

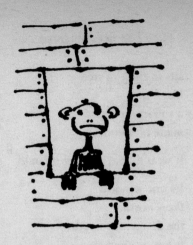

But the monkey
stares down,
scowls down
and won't descend.

He's not the boy's friend.

He was once
when his house,
his red house,
was built.

Now he smells the boy's guilt

that wafts up
to join the pain,
the phantom pain
in his tail.

And the monkey starts to wail

sending the boy
marching home,
running home
like a mouse

while the sun sets on the red house.

Bones

The horse fell in the harbour,
was splashing in the water
with the cart strapped to his back.
And a cyclist with sunglasses
and a woman with a pram
kept on going – but not the man
with the mongrel in a sack.
He dropped all and dived straight in.

The horse kept neighing
while the man was saving him
and the dog was chewing free.
Maybe the horse knew
that the man was on his way
to drown the dog. Maybe the dog
had barked this to the horse.
Oh, there were bones in the cart.

White Dog with Four Black Spots

The white dog with four black spots
is barking up the beach.
He is barking at water-skiers
and at dead baby crabs.
He tears along the sand, this way and that.
He runs into the sea, asking
'Where are the waves today?'
He barks at the stubborn sky
that keeps the sun hidden.
Most of all he barks at the children
for running away from him,
for carrying buckets of sand,
for splashing in the water.

One of the white dog's four black spots
covers his left eye. Maybe that's why
the sand-brown dog is circling
without being noticed.
There are no spots on this dog.
No sounds come from him.
He has no eyes for the sea, the sky
or the children, only the white dog
and the black spots. He wants to
bite the spots off, one by one.
He wants to bite some white off
for spots of his own. He *wants* to.

The Not So Slow Loris

The slow loris
           objected
                    to her name!
Well, she liked *loris* but not *slow*.
She was a primate too!
                    Who was man
to bandy names about?
                    What did he know,
sun-lover, long pig!
                    Let him stick
to cockroaches and kangaroos.
He didn't say *slow tortoise*.
                    He made her sick!

The slow loris
                   sat on a grave
                           and fumed!
She paid no attention to the moon
or the stupid stars —
                   man's stuff!
She wanted to go
                   into Rangoon
and complain.
                   She wanted man
to change the dictionaries.
She wanted apologies.
                   She had no plan.

The Crying Boar

The hunter sat in a pine
and watched the magnified tear
drop from the boar's eye.
He took his gun-sight away.
He was not hungry –
bacon omelettes were good
in the Gasthaus by the lake
that opened at dawn.
But good as bacon was
wild boar was better –
he drew a bead again
on the wild boar's head
and caught another tear.

Why was the boar crying?
It couldn't see the hunter
on his tree-platform,
it couldn't possibly know.
Telescopic sights
were only for hunters.
And even if it knew
why didn't it run?
Another boar-tear fell.
The hunter took his schnapps
from his bag and swigged,
shaking his hairy head.
The boar shook with sobbing
and a loud wailing
rose through the forest.
The hunter sat there
and waited till hunger returned.

Dog in Space

The barking in space
has died out now,
though dogbones rattle.
And the marks of teeth
on the sputnik's hull
are proof of a battle
impossible to win.

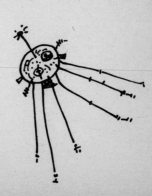

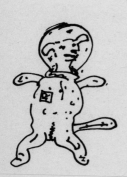

And asteroid-dents
were no help at all.
Did the dog see,
through the window,
earth's blue ball?
Did the dog know
that no other dog
had made that circle
around the earth —
her historic spin
that turned eternal?

Splat

Some days a hunk of metal
falls from the sky,
usually in the desert
or the deep, green sea.

What's it doing up there?
It's not metal litter
(which wouldn't fly!).
What could it be?

Is it bits of armour
that fell from Heaven,
or chunks of tanks
that exploded high?

Or aeroplanes of aliens
on tourist trips,
till drunken meteors
ploughed on through?

Do bones ever fall,
or the odd weird skull?
What about clothing?
A size fifty shoe?

Do birds get clobbered
as a hunk falls,
or even yachtspeople
miles out to sea?

Not to mention Piccadilly
on a Friday night.
Imagine the splat,
if the hunk wasn't shy.

Flat Bird

Forced off the pavement
by my own hurry
and three women walking abreast,
I spy a blob on the tarmac
like a map of a country
or a pattern in cement,
and as I step over it
I really look at it,
till I see what it is –
I don't want to believe it
but it's a flat bird,
a totally flat bird.

It's hard to make out
what kind of bird.
It's hard to imagine it airborne,
or having a third dimension,
or ever being heard.
Did that driver shout,
who crushed the skull,
and left the bird dead
for other drivers to flatten?
How long did it take to happen,
to make a flat bird,
a totally flat bird?

The Butcher

After his parrot escaped
the butcher stood at the door
shouting into the sky.

'Come back, parrot,' he roared
while a queue waited
for lambchops and beef,
sausages, burgers and chicken –

they could take what they liked
for all the butcher cared,
but they'd better be quick.

He got his matches out
and set fire to the shop,
then went to the airport
to fly to Venezuela

where he hired a raft
and set off down the Orinoco
with three Indian guides

who led him into a swamp
and robbed him, then killed him,
and his bones are still there
while the parrot is free.

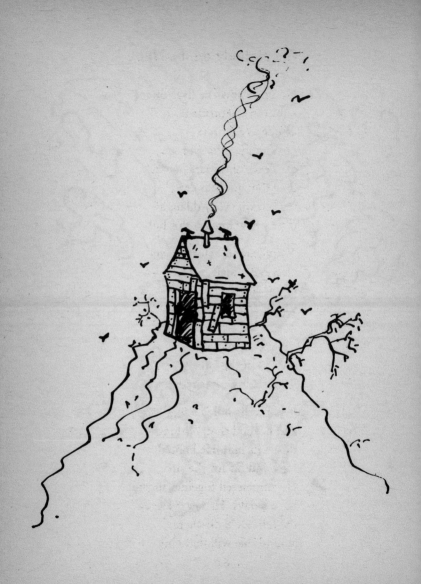

The Nobody on the Hill

No one knows he lives there,
not even the postman
as nobody writes.
His family, if he had any,
are dead, and years before
they thought him dead
for certain. They'd laugh
if they saw him on this hill.

They'd stand before his hut
and shake their heads.
Home in the city
they had a grand house,
and he lived there once.
An avenue of trees
instead of this hill.
Even their ghosts avoid it.

Beyond the hill is a bog
and beyond that, nothing –
this suits him. He hunted
long and far for the site.
He hammered together the hut
in two days. He never leaves
the hill. He'll die there
and no one will find him.

The Small Skeleton and the Big One

Beneath one skeleton was another skeleton,
and this one was smaller. And a crab
had a good home in its pelvis.

The small skeleton dreamed of swinging,
the big skeleton of walking.

The big one remembered the shark
that ate the small one and stayed hungry.
The small one remembered nuts,

and dreamed, dreamed hard of branches.
The big one dreamed of dances.

It heard again the ship's siren,
and saw the lifeboats being lowered.
The small skeleton smelled fire.

It dreamed of ropes and rooftops.
The big one dreamed of chips

or that last meal of deep-fried scampi
before he fed the shark.
The small one remembered his cage,

and dreamed of the still-locked door,
while the big one dreamed of armchairs

and the small skeleton and the big one
with flesh again, monkey and human.

Resurrected

If I got out of my grave
in a hundred years' time
I'd ignore the other risen dead
sniffing flowers, brushing their clothes,
fixing their hair, feeling their faces –
I wouldn't even read my epitaph,
but I'd make for the river
and I'd jump in, with all my clothes on,
and I'd swim, stiffly, till I was clean,
then I'd climb on the boat
waiting to take us to town.

I'd speak to nobody,
as I'd have lost the habit,
and the language would have grown.
The later dead would stare at me,
at my once-again-trendy clothes,
and of course I'd be young again
with half an eye for the women,
but first I'd head for a bar
for a long-postponed beer, and I'd
ask where a Thai restaurant was,
shining my antique coins.

Mushrooms on the Malverns

Mushrooms on the Malverns
are dropped from the moon –
why else would they appear overnight,
why else would Bismarck bark at them
and run away, or earnest walkers
(who know these hills too well)
avoid them? Their heads point up
to the unseen ball that will return
at nightfall. They are telling it
silently not to leave them here.
The brown flecks on their heads
are particles of meteorites.
They might look like mushrooms
but they are too big. Too few, also,
as if they are an expeditionary force
sent to inspect us, and to lure
a few of us into their midst
where, crouching, we'll peer at them,
then maybe run fingers down a stem
past the movable ring to the base
where a snap has the mushroom free

and moondust on your fingers
en route to your mouth. And if you
should take them home and cook them,
you will never sleep right again,
not unless you make it to the moon.

The Moon

The moon is a ball of ghosts,
    she said,
and three astronauts know
but they ain't telling. Why?
Because the ghosts insisted,
    she said,
and made the astronauts go.

For their own good, of course,
    she said
in a whispery tone of voice,
and three ghosts came with them
to Earth, then to three homes,
    she said.
The astronauts had no choice.

All three heads are grey,
    she said,
and it's no wonder. And none
is an astronaut any longer
but all three know for sure,
    she said,
they'll be back on the moon.

While I Practise My Piano

I'm being haunted by child spirits.
The door keeps opening.
Will you sit in the room with me
while I practise my piano?
You can even sing –
they won't like that,
your voice would send a bee
careering into a wall,
or would start a cat wailing.

There's the door again,
why are you so slow
at getting in here?
I've got to keep playing –
else the child spirits
will take over my piano
and play tunes of their own,
tunes that might scare me,
and once they got going
they'd never stop, so
please keep me company,
please sit in the room with me
while I practise my piano.

Ghost Eye

Mama, the ghost eye is here again –
all the way from the equator
where it lives in a dead seagull.
I'm taking my bed up to the attic
where I'll bolt myself in, Mama,
and I'm taking the robot dog with me
to guard me, my robot eye-eater.

Bubblebus

My bus will be a steel bubble
called the Bubblebus
that will roll down the empty streets
of 2010 London
where no cars will have been seen
since 1999, and only long sleek trams
will glide past me
as we stop at the bubblestops
for me to strap new passengers in.
And no one will have to pay
to ride on my bubblebus,
and no exhaust fumes
will foul London's air
because we'll be sucked along
by the huge magnets
on each terminus.
Bubblebuses, bubblebuses,
roll, roll into the near future.
I'm almost ready with the design.

Yoko Ono's Globe

was shipped in a big wooden box
from the United States.
It's 112 lbs and it's metal.
The landmasses are black,
except for the yellow coasts
that meet the blue seas.
Here and there are blobs of rust –
you know what *they* mean.
It sits on a grey, iron base
in a room in a gallery,
and Yoko Ono writes to say
she wants family events with globes,
holiday activities with globes
throughout England. I agree,
provided I get *her* globe.

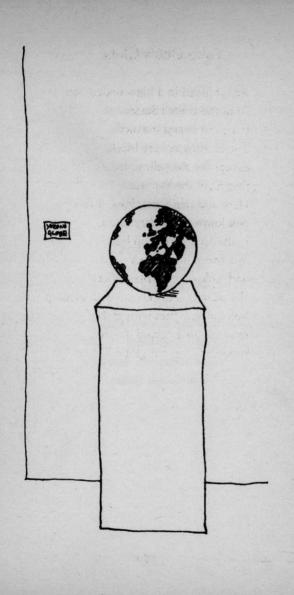

Fires

The fire I hate
is a burning planet,
a once-green ball
with nobody on it,
no animals either,
or stormy seas —
get up there, God,
put it out, please!

Some other fires
are easier to bear,
like log fires
in deepest winter,
or the private blaze
of a hate-letter —
or a dragon's breath
if we knew better.

But these good fires
are far between.
Think of cremation,
or a burning plane,
or a house on fire
with people inside,
or fire in a forest
where animals hide.

Even in barbecues
the fire's died down
before the meat
goes on to brown.
So lock the matchbox,
smash the lighter.
Keep the planet
from getting brighter.

Spotlight

Switch the spotlights on.
Make them mainly white
but have at least one red or blue.
Turn one light on each of you,
and when you're lit,
break out, have some fun –
dance, one-legged, till you sweat,
shake, collapsing in a pool,
sing a quaky, wordless song,
pretend to be a vulture,
act the ancient high-bred fool,
lie down, clap your feet,
mime a waking panther,
or a dog that's just been stung –
or any act that takes your fancy
in that round of light.
Don't stand back and crush the wall.
Don't put up a fight.
We need some wild applause,
but first we need SPOTLIGHT!

Smile

Smile, go on, smile!
Anyone would think, to look at you,
that your cat was on the barbecue
or your best friend had died.
Go on, curve your mouth.
Take a look at that beggar,
or that one-legged bus conductor.
Where's *your* cross?
Smile, slap your thigh.
Hiccup, make a horse noise,
lollop through the house,
fizz up your coffee.
Take down your guitar
from its air-shelf and play
imaginary reggae
out through the open door.
And smile, remember, smile,
give those teeth some sun,
grin at everyone,
do it now, go on, SMILE!

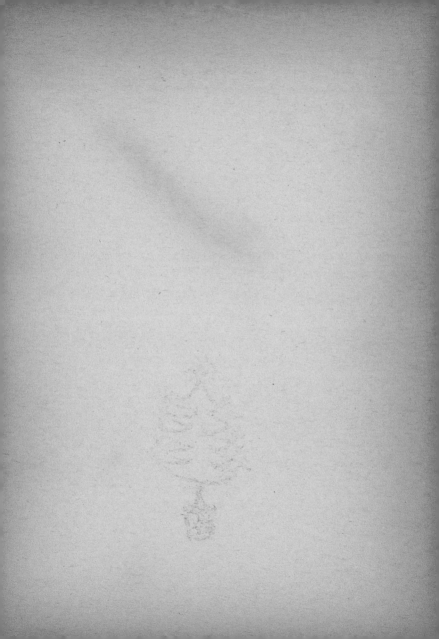